Travel America's Landmarks

Exploring Kennedy Space Center

by Emma Huddleston

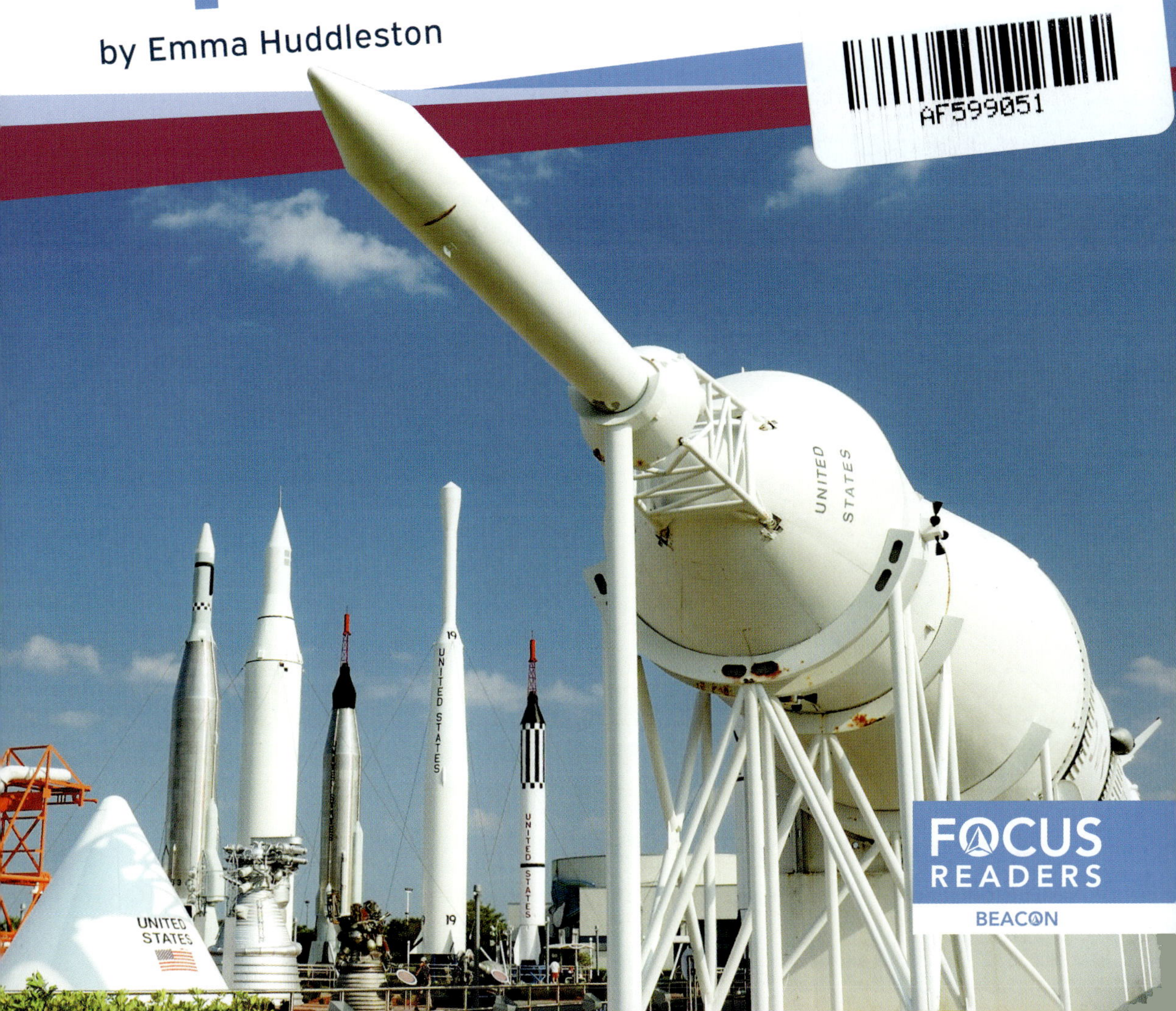

FOCUS READERS
BEACON

www.focusreaders.com

Focus Readers is distributed by North Star Editions:
sales@northstareditions.com | 888-417-0195

Produced for Focus Readers by Red Line Editorial.

Photographs ©: Purdue9394/iStockphoto, cover, 1; Allard One/Shutterstock Images, 4; achinthamb/ Shutterstock Images, 7, 27; Everett Historical/Shutterstock Images, 8, 14; AP Images, 11; KSC/ NASA, 13; MSFC/NASA, 17; JSC/NASA, 19, 29; Rui Serra Maia/Shutterstock Images, 20–21; Kelleher Photography/Shutterstock Images, 22; Red Line Editorial, 25

Library of Congress Cataloging-in-Publication Data
Names: Huddleston, Emma, author.
Title: Exploring Kennedy Space Center / by Emma Huddleston.
Description: Lake Elmo, MN : Focus Readers, [2020] | Series: Travel America's landmarks | Includes bibliographical references and index. | Audience: Grade 4 to 6.
Identifiers: LCCN 2019006356 (print) | LCCN 2019011437 (ebook) | ISBN 9781641859875 (pdf) | ISBN 9781641859233 (ebook) | ISBN 9781641857857 (hardcover) | ISBN 9781641858540 (paperback)
Subjects: LCSH: John F. Kennedy Space Center--Juvenile literature. | Outer space--Exploration--United States--History--Juvenile literature.
Classification: LCC TL4027.F52 (ebook) | LCC TL4027.F52 J639 2020 (print) | DDC 629.47/8--dc23
LC record available at https://lccn.loc.gov/2019006356

Printed in the United States of America
Mankato, MN
May, 2019

About the Author

Emma Huddleston lives in the Twin Cities with her husband. She enjoys writing children's books, but she likes reading novels even more. When she is not writing or reading, she likes to stay active by running and swing dancing. She thinks America's landmarks are fascinating and wants to visit them all!

Table of Contents

EXPLORE
Be A Part Of The Journey To Mars

Chapter 1

Exploring Space

Kennedy Space Center (KSC) is a popular **complex** in Florida. Blue letters hang over its entrance. They spell out the word "Explore." At KSC, visitors can explore US space history.

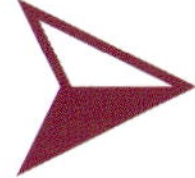

People see rockets as they enter the Kennedy Space Center.

KSC is partly a museum. People learn about famous **astronauts**. They learn about space travel. Visitors see rockets on display. They can touch the hard metal or look at a huge Saturn V.

KSC is also an active space center. People can take tours through KSC. They can learn

Saturn V is a rocket. It sent people to the moon. It is 363 feet (111 m) long.

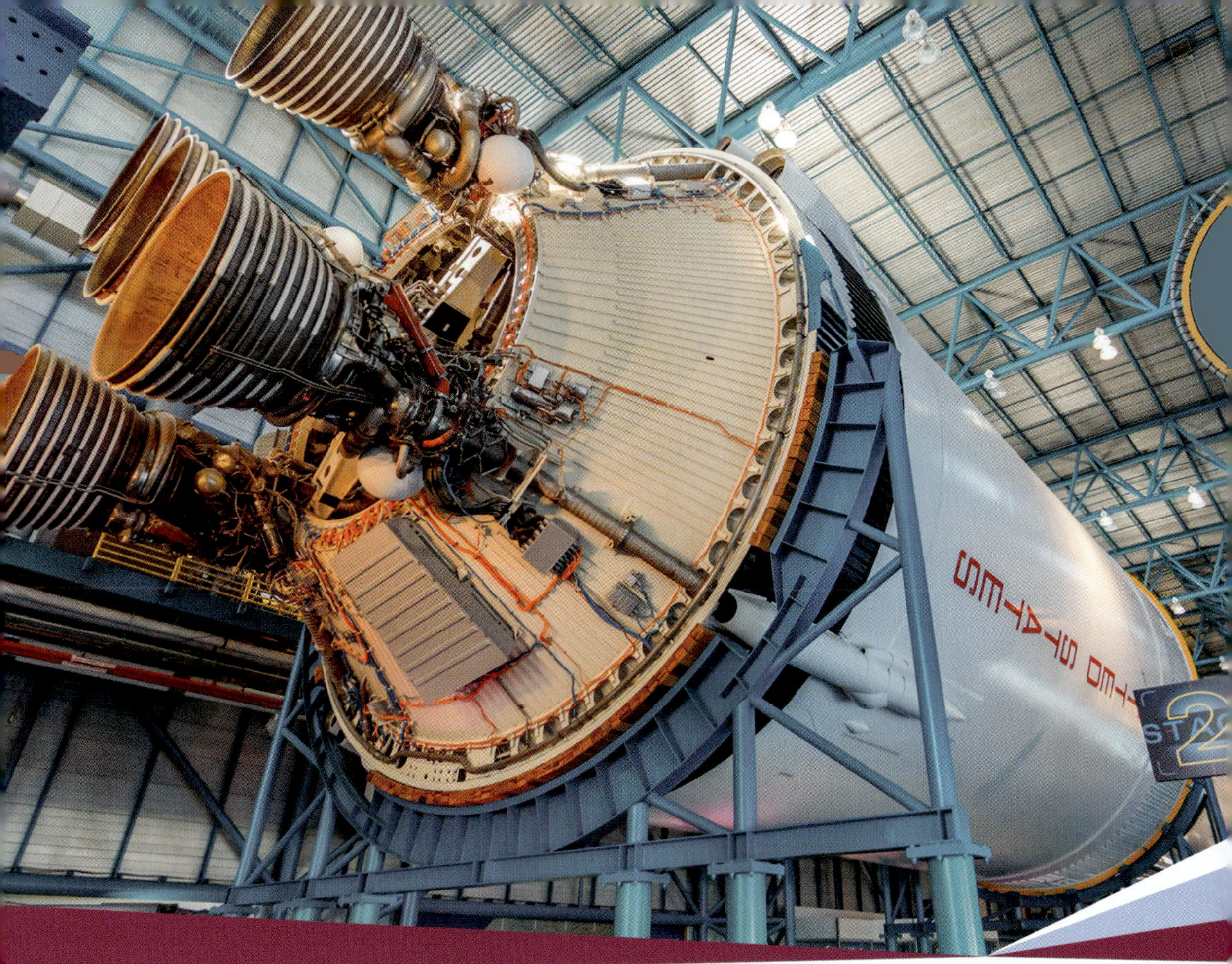

A Saturn V rocket is on display at Kennedy Space Center.

about current space **research**. They can also see key places in US space history, such as historic **launch** sites.

Chapter 2

Space Race

Space research took off in the 1950s and 1960s. The United States was racing the Soviet Union. The United States wanted to be the first country to land on the moon.

The takeoff of *Friendship 7* in 1962 helped prepare the United States for its later moon landing.

In 1958, the US government created **NASA**. This organization directed nonmilitary space activity. It built rockets. It trained astronauts. Its goal was to explore space.

NASA had many centers in the United States. But it needed a good launch site. The US army launched rockets from Cape Canaveral. This base is in Florida. NASA bought the land nearby. It created a space center in 1962. The center was

President John F. Kennedy (center) attends a talk on NASA's moon-landing program in 1963.

named Kennedy Space Center in 1963. It was named after President John F. Kennedy.

At first, KSC had no visitor center. People could only drive by the area. Even so, driving tours were popular.

Many people wanted to see where rockets were launched. In 1966, official bus tours began. More than 475,000 people took a bus tour in the first year.

In 1967, the first visitor center opened. But before long, it was too small to fit all the visitors. KSC added buildings. Rockets went on

In 1969, KSC was the second-most popular place to visit in Florida.

Former president Lyndon B. Johnson (center) watches the launch of Apollo 11 from KSC.

display. Restaurants opened. Bus tours increased. Visitors learned about US space history.

Chapter 3

Space Missions

Kennedy Space Center is a base for US space travel. Cape Canaveral is nearby. It is one of NASA's main launch sites. Many of NASA's historic moments took place there.

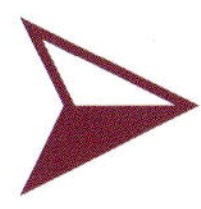

Cape Canaveral is a US Air Force station. NASA launches some of its rockets there.

In 1961, Alan Shepard left Earth in the *Freedom 7* spacecraft. He was the first US astronaut in space.

The 1967 Apollo 1 mission was tragic. The rocket caught on fire. The crew died. A **memorial** was later built at KSC. It honors astronauts who have died.

The US space program grew a lot during the 1960s. NASA sent astronauts to space in 22 successful missions.

NASA watches the progress of its space missions from control centers around the United States.

NASA had several successful missions. In 1968, *Apollo 8* became the first spacecraft to **orbit** the moon. Then, in 1969, the Apollo 11 mission took people to the moon.

Neil Armstrong and Buzz Aldrin walked on the moon.

NASA continues to build new rockets. The Space Launch System is a deep space rocket. It is NASA's first since the Saturn V. It will launch from KSC. It will send people to the moon. NASA also

Rockets send spacecraft into space. But rockets do not stay in space. They fall back to Earth.

Astronaut Buzz Aldrin walks on the surface of the moon during the Apollo 11 mission.

plans to send people to Mars. It will send a mission to one of Jupiter's moons, too.

THAT'S AMAZING!

Merritt Island National Wildlife Refuge

NASA had extra land left over when it built KSC. So, it worked with the US Fish and Wildlife Service to create a National Wildlife **Refuge**.

The refuge is a place that protects wildlife. More than 1,500 kinds of plants and animals live there. Some of the plants and animals are **endangered**.

Hiking and fishing are popular activities at the refuge. Visitors see animals in nature. They learn about many kinds of wildlife.

The National Wildlife Refuge is home to many flocks of birds.

HEROES
AND
LEGENDS
UNITED STATES
ASTRONAUT HALL OF FAME
BOEING

Chapter 4

Visiting Kennedy Space Center

Kennedy Space Center has many areas to visit. People can explore another planet in the Journey to Mars area. They can learn about astronauts in the Heroes and Legends building.

The Heroes and Legends building includes the US Astronaut Hall of Fame.

The Mission Zones museum teaches about US space history. It shows pictures and items from historic missions. The NASA Now and Next area shows plans for future missions. Someday, astronauts will go deep into space. They will land on Mars.

The Lunch with an Astronaut program began in 2000. Today, visitors can still meet with astronauts.

An astronaut training center opened in 2017. Visitors sit in chairs that move. The ride feels like a rocket taking off.

Bus tours travel to Cape Canaveral. There are launch pads along the Atlantic Ocean. Visitors see where NASA's first rocket launched. On another tour, people visit the Vehicle Assembly Building (VAB). Rockets and space shuttles are **assembled** there.

The VAB is one of the world's largest buildings. The Space Launch System will be assembled there.

The Vehicle Assembly Building is large enough to hold rockets.

Finally, NASA continues to send missions into space. Many space launches happen during the year at KSC. People can buy tickets to see them. KSC will remain a key center that supports US space travel.

FOCUS ON

KENNEDY SPACE CENTER

Write your answers on a separate piece of paper.

1. Write a letter to a friend describing the historic space missions at Kennedy Space Center.
2. Which part of Kennedy Space Center would you want to see first? Why?
3. Who became the first US astronaut in space in 1961?
   - **A.** Alan Shepard
   - **B.** Buzz Aldrin
   - **C.** Neil Armstrong
4. Why did NASA create and later expand its visitor center at Kennedy Space Center?
   - **A.** Many people wanted to visit the center.
   - **B.** People stopped going on the driving tours.
   - **C.** NASA needed money to continue its work.

5. What does **tragic** mean in this book?

The 1967 Apollo 1 mission was ***tragic****. The rocket caught on fire. The crew died.*

- **A.** delayed or postponed
- **B.** terrible or unfortunate
- **C.** successful or productive

6. What does **historic** mean in this book?

The Mission Zones museum teaches about US space history. It shows pictures and items from ***historic*** *missions.*

- **A.** related to space
- **B.** forgotten over time
- **C.** important in history

Answer key on page 32.

Glossary

assembled
Put together.

astronauts
People who are trained to work or travel in space.

complex
A group of buildings on the same site.

endangered
In danger of dying out.

launch
To start or set in motion.

memorial
A structure built to remind people of a specific person or event.

NASA
The National Aeronautics and Space Administration.

orbit
To repeatedly follow a curved path around another object because of gravity.

refuge
An area of land where animals are protected from hunting.

research
The act of studying something to learn more about it.

To Learn More

BOOKS

Aldrin, Buzz, and Marianne J. Dyson. *To the Moon and Back*. Washington, DC: National Geographic Kids, 2018.

Doudna, Kelly. *Space Exploration*. Minneapolis: Abdo Publishing, 2017.

Orr, Tamra B. *Space Discoveries*. North Mankato, MN: Capstone Press, 2019.

NOTE TO EDUCATORS

Visit **www.focusreaders.com** to find lesson plans, activities, links, and other resources related to this title.

Index

Answer Key: 1. Answers will vary; **2.** Answers will vary; **3.** A; **4.** A; **5.** B; **6.** C